Down to the Sea

The Story of
A Little Salmon and His Neighborhood

Text and Illustrations
Jay W. Nicholas

BookPartners
Wilsonville, Oregon

Library of Congress Cataloging-in-Publication Data

Nicholas, Jay W.
    Down to the sea : the story of a little salmon and his neighborhood / Jay Nicholas.
       p.   cm.
    Summary: A little fish learns the spirit of Oregon's plan to protect coho salmon.
    ISBN 1-58151-038-1 (hardcover : alk. paper). --Isbn 1-58151-036-5 (pbk. : alk. paper)
    [1. Salmon Fiction.   2. Wildlife conservation Fiction.   3. Watershed management Fiction.   4. Environmental protection Fiction.   5. Oregon Fiction.]   I. Title.
PZ7.N5117Do   1999
[Fic]--dc21

99-32665
CIP

Cover design by Richard Ferguson
Text design by Sheryl Mehary

BookPartners, Inc.
P. O. Box 922
Wilsonville, Oregon 97070

Dedication

To all the little fish of the world …

… especially to my boys David and Jackson

Down to the Sea

The Story of
A Little Salmon and
His Neighborhood

It started one May morning in 1997.

I was walking along the sandy tideflats near the mouth of a small Oregon coastal river, and I was worried. Worried about salmon. Worried that there were so few of them in Oregon rivers these days. Many of our rivers had once been home to thousands and thousands of salmon. Coho salmon, chum salmon, chinook salmon, sockeye salmon, and steelhead too.

Birds ate them. Otters, seals, and bears ate them. People ate them. And people loved them too. Salmon were a big part of the circle of life in Oregon, the fabric of our communities.

But not now. These were hard times for salmon in many parts of Oregon, hard times for people who loved salmon.

So I had come here, to this river, this place where I had wandered as a boy, imagining days when these waters were rich with salmon.

I left the city behind me, pulled on my old rubber boots, bundled up in my red wool coat, and wandered along the shore, listening to the splash of little wavelets, smelling the salt air, searching shallow water for signs of life.

Eventually, I wound up on my hands and knees, looking at ripples in the sand, admiring the uncountable squiggles and holes made by critters of some kind, hiding under the surface.

As I neared the river's edge, a coho salmon smolt squirted out of the water and landed, flip-flopping, right under my nose.

Needless to say, I was startled, but I quickly went about trying to gather up the little fish in my hands and get him back in the water. Well, my rescue effort did not go smoothly. What with his wiggling and my cold fingers, it took a long time to get a hold of him. By the time I had cupped him in my hands, he was barely twitching, and I was alarmed to see silvery traces of his scales and protective slime, scattered about the area where he landed.

So instead of just tossing him back into the river, I knelt in the shallows and submerged my hands, letting all four inches of him rest there, hoping he would be okay if he could rest for awhile. He was on his side, his gills pumping furiously to catch his breath.

As I peered into the water, watching him, I thought I could hear a faint voice saying...

"Will you help me please?"

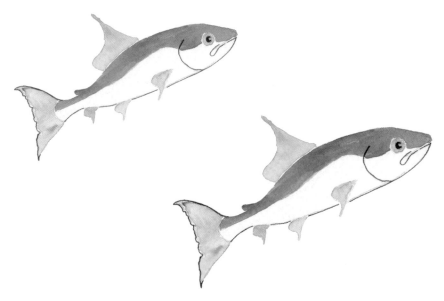

I looked around me, but there was only a seagull watching, no doubt hoping for a tasty morning snack.

Returning my attention to the wounded fish, I heard the voice again, a little stronger now, "Will you help me? Please?"

"Huh?" I replied, articulate as ever.

"Are you talking to me, little smolt?" I said, knowing that fish can't really talk, but wishing they could.

"Why yes, I am talking to you."

I was taken aback by the little talking salmon, but decided to answer him.

"So, what kind of help did you have in mind, little fish?"

"We salmon need help from people—help to keep our neighborhoods safe."

"Your neighborhoods?"

"Yes. You know, the river reaches where we are born, where we grow up and prepare for our migration to the sea, where we return to spawn, and finally, where we will die and enrich the earth."

"Oh," I said, "you mean your watersheds."

"Sure, sure," the little salmon said, "you can call them whatever you want, but it's our neighborhoods that we need help with. Can you, will you, help us?"

"Well, yes," I said. "In fact, this just happens to be your lucky day, little fish. You see, a lot of people have been working on a new *plan,* a whole new way of helping salmon."

"Oh, thank goodness," the little fish said. "I have been sent by all my brothers and sisters to ask for help, real help, keeping our neighborhoods safe. I have been making my smolt migration to the ocean from the little tributary where I was born and lived. When I saw you kneeling by my river, I knew you were the one to talk to."

"Well," I said, flattered, "why don't you tell me about the problems in your neighborhood."

"Well, for instance," he said, "if people cut too many trees near the water's edge, there may not be enough shade and the water may get too warm in the summer. And if you take all the bends and curves out of our streams and haul all the big logs out of the pools—the water might be too swift and prevent us from finding shelter during the winter storms. And if people are not careful about how they build culverts under roads, they may block our way to the tributaries where we spawn or shelter in the winter. And if people are not careful, your roads may tumble into our streams, and leave too much mud in the gravel. And if you are not careful about how you dispose of the waste from your houses and industries, and the chemicals you use to care for your crops and your lawns, the water we live in may not be safe for us or for people. And if people…"

"Okay, okay," I said. "We have those things covered in our plan to help salmon. In fact, if you don't mind waiting, I can drive back to town and get a complete copy of The Plan for you and your salmon friends to share."

"Wow, that's wonderful," said the little fish. "But before you go, could you please tell me if your plan recognizes that fishermen sometimes have caught too many salmon with nets and hooks?"

"Well, yes, it does," I said. "And The Plan also recognizes that some of our efforts to produce salmon in hatcheries have probably hurt salmon more than they have helped."

"What about the dams?" asked the little fish. "Does your plan say much about dams?"

"Well, we do note that many big and little dams and irrigation diversions have made it difficult for salmon to migrate upstream and downstream, and that people need to work together to fix these problems."

"Great!" said the little salmon. "Now, why don't you get on your way and bring a copy of The Plan to me as quickly as you can."

"Okay," I said. "It will take a couple of hours to get back to my office and copy nearly 3,000 pages. It shouldn't take more than half a day, then there's the index tabbing, hole punching, buying the binders…. Why, I should be able to get back here by low tide about this time tomorrow!"

"*I* don't think you quite understand. You see, I am just a little fish, and I really can't handle all that paper in those heavy binders. Can't you boil it down for me?" The little smolt righted himself now, and, leaving the shelter of my hands, stirred up little grains of sand in the water with his fins.

"Oh, yes. Of course. How silly of me. Of course you don't need the whole Plan. A lot of it is technical and administrative documentation. Some of it is repetitious. It is all useful in some way, but you needn't see it all. Goodness no, you don't need to see it all to get the real meaning of The Plan."

Jay Nicholas©1997

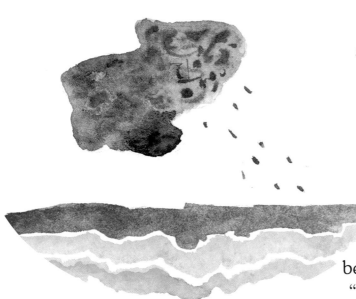

"What if I get you a copy of volume 1?" I suggested. "It isn't much over an inch thick, and it fits in a single binder. It reviews the history of how the salmon problem developed over the last century, summarizes key elements of The Plan, and highlights some real obstacles to solving the salmon problem."

"Hello-o!" the little fish said, sounding a trifle irate, and looking quite feisty again. His back was a brilliant blue-green, his belly the cleanest cloud-white you will ever see.

"You don't seem to be getting the picture. I am just a little fish. I can't cope with one binder any better than with four. Can't you boil it down for me?"

"Oh. I see," I said. "I'm so very sorry. Yes, of course I can boil it down. We have a very nice executive summary that is less than twenty pages, with an illustration of a coho on the cover, and maps and charts. It's sort of an overview of the whole plan."

"Well, maybe I could handle the executive summary," the little smolt said, bravely.

"Great! In fact, I happen to have a copy in my briefcase right here that I can give you."

So I pulled out a summary and showed it to the little coho. I talked about how The Plan will help salmon. I mentioned the voluntary contributions by Oregon grassroots organizations, private landowners, and the timber industry. I noted that fishing seasons had almost been eliminated. I tried to explain how important it was that state and federal agencies were cooperating better than ever before to improve conditions for salmon. Finally, I told him that Oregon had promised to monitor the results and to improve The Plan in the future.

The little salmon appreciated what I told him, but I could see that he was getting a little fidgety.

"I really must be getting on with my migration," he said. "If you would be so kind as to give me the summary, I will take it to study with my fellow salmon. We will learn all the important features of the great plan as we go about our life at sea."

Seeing that the little smolt was looking quite strong now, I took a long piece of eel grass and gently tied the executive summary to his tail.

Much to my disappointment, the little fish couldn't even budge the summary, no matter how hard he tugged against the eelgrass tether. All he accomplished was to stir up a cloud of sand and dig a little depression in the shallow bottom of the river.

"Maybe I could boil it down more," I said, untying the little fish. "Maybe, if I really, really boil it down, I might be able to describe The Plan on a single piece of paper."

The little smolt was looking rather frazzled and settled down to rest on the waterlogged summary. Grains of sand and little sand creatures settled onto the surface of the paper. The ink was starting to run, blurring the words on the cover.

I realized then that I was going to have to boil down The Plan even more, figure out just what the most important elements were, and write them down for the little fish.

So while he caught his breath, I pulled out my laptop, set it down in the water so he could see the screen while I typed, and began to write.

The whole plan.

On a single piece of paper.

Over a year in the making. State and federal agencies. Private landowners. Local governments. Scientists. Industry. Conservation groups. The Governor. The Legislature. School children. Hundreds, no, thousands of people contributing.

The future of salmon in Oregon, some say, is at stake.

Boiled down to a single piece of paper.

Quite a task.

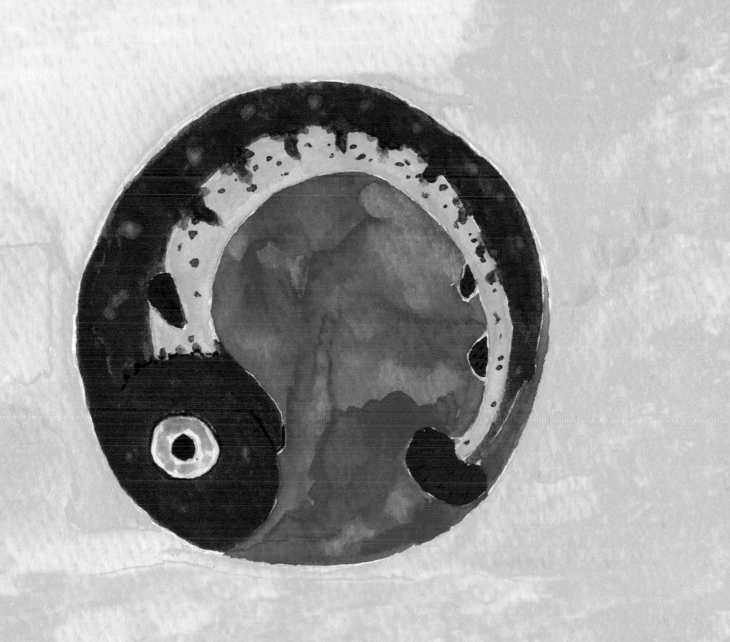

The tidal water was cold. Every once in a while, a wave rolled over the top of my hip boots as I knelt there in the shallows. The pockets of my faded wool coat were dragging in the river. The little salmon moved around under me in the water, finning over the keyboard as I typed, watching intently as words appeared on the half-submerged screen. Sometimes I bumped him as I reached for the mouse with my thumb.

"Excuse me," I muttered, and went on typing.

Beads of sweat stood out on my forehead. The little fish was mostly quiet, turning his head from side to side, reading as I worked. Sometimes, when I used a very big word, he asked me to explain what I meant. Once he asked me to tilt the screen a little, to ease the glare. The little salmon was very patient.

My back was cramped and my fingers were cold, wrinkled up by the salt water. Finally I was finished.

The whole plan.

On a single page.

Jay Nicholas
© 1997

"I think I understand," said the little fish. "But it is still quite a lot to digest. I think that I'd better take this summary with me so I can study it, think about it, and let it sink in for awhile."

"Wonderful!" I said, and started to set up my portable printer in the water beside the laptop. Naturally, I used waterproof paper. In an instant, I was securing the single piece of paper to the little fish's tail.

"Thanks! I've got to be going now. My ocean rearing phase is calling." And the little fish swam off.

That is, he tried to.

Even though it was only a single sheet of paper, it foundered the little fish, and soon he was struggling at the surface, not making any headway at all.

Mr. Seagull, who had been watching us with a hungry eye, saw the little fish at the surface and swooped down at him. The tiny smolt escaped at the last moment only by hiding under the paper.

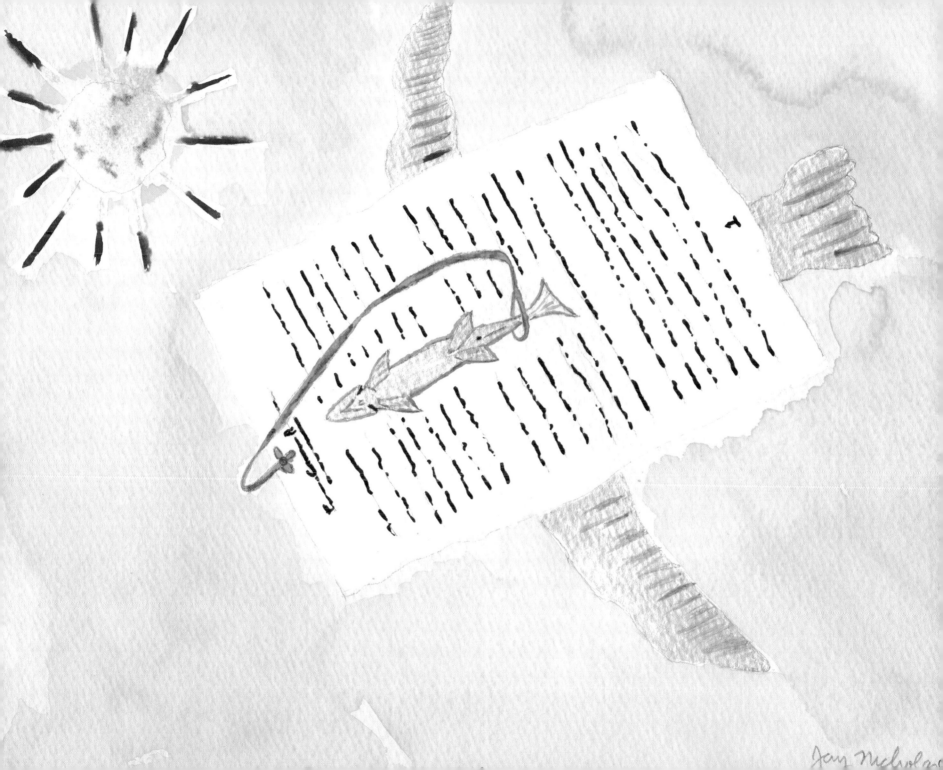

Jay Nicholas

I chased Mr. Seagull off and retrieved the little fish, freeing him from his burden. I sat there with him up to my armpits in the water. Neither of us spoke for quite a while.

"I don't suppose that you could boil it down any more?" said the little fish.

It was a question. I had no answer.

Faintly now, he continued. "I, …we, … salmon will understand that you have tried." He sighed. "I must be going now."

The incoming tide was surging up to my neck.

"I really must be going. Now."

And then it came to me.

Like a bolt of lightning out of the sky, for the first time I understood the true meaning of The Plan. The great new plan to help keep watersheds safe for salmon.

It wasn't just about government agencies working together, or about ordinary people volunteering to make changes to help salmon. It wasn't just about harvest regulations, or changing hatchery programs, or working to improve water quality or restoring complexity to stream channels and wetlands, or even about scientific review of results.

It was more basic than all of that.

It was about salmon, yes, and about people too.

It was about planning for the future. The future of salmon *and* people.

"Wait!" I shouted. "Give me one more chance."

The current was swirling around us. My face was completely under water to see the screen.

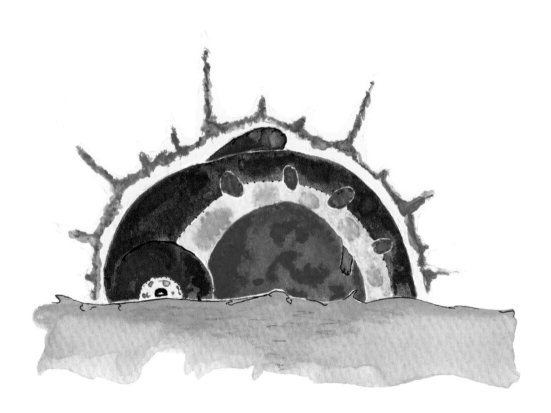

Staghorn sculpin were chasing little sand bugs hiding in the keyboard.

I had only one single sentence to write. One sentence to describe Oregon's salmon conservation plan.

A pledge.

When I was finished, I slipped a single fine thread of eelgrass into the printer, and pushed the print key.

The little salmon was swimming in circles around the printer, hiding from a cutthroat trout who clearly wanted to eat him. When the eelgrass emerged from the printer, the little salmon caught one end of it on a tooth in the corner of his mouth. It lay so smoothly against his side that it was no burden at all.

"Wow! Yippee!" The little smolt shouted, and dashed off into the estuary with his very own copy of The Oregon Plan.

I called to him. "Wait! Remember that is just an unofficial draft! I need to take it back to the office and send it out for review by the technical staff, the policy experts, and the political advisors."

But the little salmon was gone now, off on the rest of his life journey.

"You do your part, and I'll do mine," the little salmon shouted over his shoulder, leaping through the surf.

I felt around in the sand for my laptop, but I couldn't find it. Ghost shrimp were already laying eggs in the keyboard. A one-armed crab pinched at my fingers as I groped around in the murky water.

The printer washed ashore with a surge of the tide. And Mr. Seagull perched on it. He startled as I lumbered out of the river, lifted his wings, pooped *mightily* on the printer, and flew off.

I turned again and shouted at the ocean, "Don't you want to know if coho salmon were listed under the Endangered Species Act?"

Apparently, the little salmon did not hear me.

The waves washed away my footprints as I made my way to shore, hissing as they followed me across the flats.

I didn't have a copy of the pledge I had given the little salmon. But I didn't need it. Even I could remember the one-sentence version of the great new plan, The Oregon Plan for Salmon and Watersheds.

We, the people of Oregon,
promise to do our best to understand
and respect the needs of salmon
and to make some change in the way
we live our daily lives, in the hope
that both salmon and people
will survive and flourish
in the future.

The End

The Life Cycle of Salmon

*I*t is important if we are to help salmon survive and replenish their numbers, to understand how they are born, live and die.

Coho, the species to which the little salmon smolt belonged, is recognized by the small spots on the back and upper tail-fin lobe. Young coho, like the little smolt, stay in fresh water for about a year before entering North Pacific waters. They grow into adults in about three years and return in fall or winter to the stream where they were born.

There, the females dig nests, called redds, in stream gravel with their tails. Males fertilize the eggs as they are deposited in the nests. The female then covers the eggs with gravel to protect them from winter floods and predators.

After spawning—the egg laying and fertilizing process—all coho salmon die. Their bodies provide nourishment for fish, birds, mammals, invertebrates, and plants in the watershed—the salmon's neighborhood.

The new generation of salmon is called alevins. These tiny future fish hatch from eggs laid in the gravel and remain there for a while, living off the nutrients in their yolk sacs, learning to feed.

Sac fry—the next stage—emerge from the gravel in the spring and live along the stream margins in relatively calm water while they continue to learn to feed and grow stronger.

Parr—the next step in the growing cycle—live in the streams during the remainder of the summer, gradually moving into deeper water as they grow. Older youngsters, called juvenile coho, usually live in fairly small streams and tend to prefer pools. In the winter, juvenile coho need to find shelter from floods that could sweep them downstream into the ocean before they have grown large enough to survive.

Young coho begin to smolt during spring when they are about a year old. Smolts tend to have bluish backs and silvery sides and have reached the stage where they are ready to survive in the ocean.

Smolts enter the ocean and move offshore seeking food, migrating along genetically determined routes that may encompass thousands of miles. Then, in two years or so when they reach maturity, they return to the river where they were born.

As silvery adults homing in to their native rivers, coho salmon migrate upstream, gradually turning to hues of red, brown, and black as hormone balances change preparing them for spawning.

The egg laying and fertilizing signals the birthing of a new generation and the dying of the old.

— Thorn Bacon

Acknowledgments

Many people helped bring this book from my imagination to the printing press. My family helped me find the courage to begin painting long after I had decided that "I didn't know how."

The idea of publishing the book to benefit children and salmon was transformed into reality by Mim Swartz of the Oregon Youth Conservation Corps, with support from the Oregon Wildlife Heritage Foundation. Proceeds from sales will be used to support OYCC programs for youth.

The preparation of this book was funded in part with a grant from the Oregon State Lottery through the Strategic Reserve Fund administered by the State of Oregon Economic and Community Development Department.

You Can Help

Support the Oregon Youth Conservation Corps programs and efforts to save salmon and watersheds. For information on how you can help, write to:

Oregon Youth Conservation Corps
1201 Court Street, N.E., Suite 302
Salem, Oregon 97301
or call: (503) 378-3441

The Oregon Wildlife Heritage Foundation is working to improve fish and wildlife by restoring watersheds throughout Oregon. This work is supported by partnerships with private landowners, watershed councils, soil and water conservation districts, government agencies, businesses, outdoor enthusiasts, and various funding sources. For more information, write:

Oregon Wildlife Heritage Foundation
P.O. Box 30406
Portland, Oregon 97294-3406
or call: (503) 255-6059

To order additional copies of

Down to the Sea: The Story of a Little Salmon and His Neighborhood

Hardback Book: $35.00   Shipping/Handling: $3.50
Paperback Book: $15.00   Shipping/Handling: $3.50

Contact: **BookPartners, Inc.**
P.O. Box 922
Wilsonville, OR 97070

E-mail: bpbooks@teleport.com
Fax: 503-682-8684
Phone: 503-682-9821
Order: 1-800-895-7323

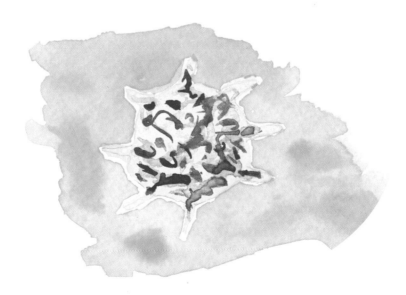

Jay Nicholas 199-

Special Thanks to:

OYCC Advisory Committee and Corporate Board
Oregon Wildlife Heritage Foundation
Jackson County Soil and Water Conservation District
Oregon Department of Fish and Wildlife
Fish Restoration and Enhancement Program
Governor's Watershed Enhancement Board
Oregon Department of Agriculture
Electro Scientific Industries
Starker Forests Inc.
Oregon Trout
Gary and Paulett Graham
Rose Marie Davis
Mabel L. Bishop
Paul McCracken
Judy Uherbelau
Weston Becker
Jerry G. Jones
Jeff Pampush
Rod Brobeck
Kim MaColl
Bart Starker